BUFFALO
BERT

Michaela Morgan

Illustrated by Ian Newsham

White Wolves Series Consultant: Sue Ellis,
Centre for Literacy in Primary Education

This book can be used in the White Wolves Guided Reading programme
with Year 3 children who have an average level of reading experience

Reprinted 2006, 2008
First published 2004 by
A & C Black Publishers Ltd
38 Soho Square, London, W1D 3HB

www.acblack.com

Text copyright © 2004 Michaela Morgan
Illustrations copyright © 2004 Ian Newsham

The rights of Michaela Morgan and Ian Newsham to be
identified as author and illustrator of this work respectively
have been asserted by them in accordance with the
Copyrights, Designs and Patents Act 1988.

ISBN 978-0-7136-6863-6

A CIP catalogue for this book is available from the British Library.

This book is produced using paper that is made from wood grown in
managed, sustainable forests. It is natural, renewable and recyclable.
The logging and manufacturing processes conform to the
environmental regulations of the country of origin.

Printed and bound in Great Britain by
CPI Cox & Wyman, Reading, RG1 8EX

Contents

To Tom

Chapter One

They call me Sunny...

... but I'm not feeling very
bright and sunny at the moment.
You see, I've got a problem.

Here he is.

He's my grandad.

cowboy hat

Cowboy
shirt

Cowboy
belt

Cowboy
boots

Spurs

I call him Gramps. But he calls himself…

Buffalo Bert
the fastest grandad in the
Wild West Road

He thinks he's a cowboy.
A cowboy grandad!

Buffalo Bert! Huh! I don't
think he's ever seen a buffalo.
He's never even been near a
buffalo. He does sound
a bit like one
when he's
snoring.

I used to think my gramps
was fantastic!
He used to tell
me cowboy
bedtime stories.

He used to
sing me
cowboy
bedtime songs.

We used
to have fun
in the park.
I used to
LOVE it!

But now I'm big I say:
"Don't be silly, Gramps" or
"Grow up, Gramps" and "Act
your age!"

I bet *your* grandad doesn't
wear a cowboy belt, a cowboy
shirt and boots with spurs that
jingle-jangle-jingle?

I bet your grandad doesn't wear a cowboy hat with a big feather in it, like this?

I bet people don't point and stare at your grandad.

When people point at Gramps do you know what he does?

He just tips his hat and says, "Howdy!"

Chapter Two

I know what a proper grandad should be like. I've seen them on the telly and in books.

They have pink cheeks, a snowy beard and they spend their time snoozing quietly in an armchair.

They might have a pipe. They probably wear slippers. They are quiet.

My gramps is not quiet.

He sings…

He dances. He strums a guitar and he makes up his own songs.

Having a cowboy grandad is a problem for me.

You see, I've only been at my new school for three weeks now. I want to fit in. I want to be just like all the other kids.

Everyone has been friendly – but they are all very cool. Super cool. Mega cool.

Not one of them has a grandad who shouts, **"Yeehah!"** when he goes into the post office.

Chapter Three

I've got three best friends at the moment. They are Kirsty, Binni and Nick.

I've been to each of their houses. I've had tea. I've watched telly at their houses.

I've played computer games and I've noticed not one of them has a cowboy grandad. It's just not normal.

It's my turn to invite them to my house. I know exactly what I should do. I should invite them all at the same time (it will be more fun that way).

I should get Mum to give them sausages, chips and beans and some special ice cream (they will all *love* that).

Then we will all watch telly (we all love cartoons). Easy!

But if I bring friends home they will meet my gramps. I love my gramps, but I can imagine what will happen.

He'll make them join in his latest line dance.

He'll make terrible jokes. He'll *sing* to them and he'll be wearing a purple shirt, cowboy boots, his cowboy belt and that hat.

How embarrassing will that be?

What can I do?

Chapter Four

I made a list of plans.

1. Leave the country

2. Change school

3. Try to get Gramps out of the house while my friends are there.

I decided to go for plan Number 3.

The next time we were in the library I took Gramps over to the noticeboard and pointed out all the things he could do.

I wanted Gramps to take up a hobby that would keep him out of the house.

"There are millions of clubs you can join," I told him.

"There are loads of things to do. There are meetings, talks, visits."

"Hmm..." he said.

"What about a visit to the Old Timers' Drop-in Centre?" I suggested.

He shook his head.

"Or how about going to the Old Age Pensioners' Tea Party?" I said.

He yawned.

"Well why not go to this talk called 'Looking after your Toenails?'" I suggested.

He didn't look keen.

I didn't give up. "What about 'Paper Folding For Fun and Profit' or 'Keep Slim and Beautiful' or 'The History of Cheese'?"

He said he didn't think so.

"Well, how about 'All you Need to Know about Keeping a Goat' or 'First Steps in Ballet' or … 'Make your own Shoes'?"

I was getting desperate. He gave me a funny look. And in the end I told him the truth.

"I don't want you to be in the house when my friends come to tea. You're different to all the other grandads – it's embarrassing."

"Oh," he said.

He looked a little sad.

"I see," he said and he blew his nose.

"You're ashamed of me…" he said and he sighed.

We walked home in silence. Gramps didn't **yahoo** or pretend to be riding a horse. He just trudged along quietly.

"Are you OK, Gramps?"
I asked.

"Just thinking," he said. And
he sighed.

When we got home he sat
down in his favourite chair.

Then he said, "I'll keep out
of the way when your friends
are here. There's plenty of
work to do in the garden. You
won't even know I'm here."

He went up to his room.
I heard him singing quietly...

They call me Buffalo,
Buffalo Bert.
With my cowboy hat and boots,
My cowboy belt and shirt.
I'm a hard-headed cowboy,
But I can still be hurt.
That's the sad truth about
Buffalo Bert.

I felt a bit bad about Gramps – but I felt really pleased that now everything would be just right when my friends came!

I wanted everything to be PERFECT.

Chapter Five

At last Thursday came round
– and so did my friends.

In they came. Binni
glanced at the television.
"Don't you have a DVD?"
she asked.

Kirsty looked at the sofa "We used to have one like this," she said.

"Can I play on your computer?" Nick asked.

I had to admit I hadn't got one.

Oh dear. It wasn't going well. But then Mum popped in.

"I'm making sausages, chips, beans and ... there's a very special surprise," she said.

"Mmm, sausages!" said Nick. I knew the surprise was going to be nutty toffee ice cream with chocolate sauce so I started to relax. Everything was going to be fine.

It was then that I spotted them – the photographs!

There, framed and on display were:

A picture of me as a baby wearing only a sunhat and a huge toothless grin.

 A picture of me in a paddling pool wearing only orange blow-up armbands.

A picture of me running round in a nappy and carrying a toy ducky.

Three terrible pictures
perched on the window sill!

Binni, Kirsty and Nick
hadn't spotted them yet, so I
pushed my three friends on to
the sofa, jumped past them,
grabbed the pictures and
shoved them behind the
curtains quickly.

Just as well! Through the curtains I could see Gramps.

He was wearing his cowboy shirt, his cowboy hat – the works. He was building a bonfire of garden rubbish and he was singing quietly to himself.

Sometimes it's hard to be a grandad.

Doing all you can to just get by.

Then little Sunny,

Tells you you're funny,

And you feel so sad that you could cry.

I slammed the window shut, grabbed the curtains and closed them before my gramps could be seen.

"It's better to watch telly in the dark," I said and I switched the telly on quickly and turned it up before they could hear Gramps's singing.

My friends looked a bit
surprised but Nick smiled.
"Just in time for the cartoons!"
he said.

But no. The cartoons were
off. Disaster.

Everything interesting was
off. All the television channels
were given over to some "News
Special".

"Oh no!" said Binni and
Nick.

"Now what?" said Kirsty.

We all peered at the telly and zapped from channel to channel.

News, news or more news.

There was nothing for us to watch. Not one thing.

Binni sighed. "Don't you have digital? Or cable? Or satellite?" she asked.

"No," I admitted.

"Boring." Nick muttered.

"Maybe we could go into the garden?" suggested Kirsty.

"NO!" I shouted. "I mean, it's too cold. And it gets dark early at this time of year. Let's just stay here."

We all slumped on the sofa and gazed at the telly. My friends looked at each other. Then they looked at me.

"It's boring without telly,"
said Nick. "Boring. Boring.
Boring!"

Then, "What's that noise?"
asked Kirsty.

Grandad's singing was
getting louder. Now he was
yodelling...

Yodellaayyaaaa

"It's a ... a ... a ... chicken!"
I stuttered. I couldn't think of
anything better and he *did*
sound like an animal in pain.

"Have you got chickens in the garden?" said Binni. "Ooh let's go and see them."

"NO!" I yelled, "they're … going to bed. That's their bedtime noise … They always sort of … cluck and … yodel … and sing … before they go to bed."

Everyone went quiet and listened.

Then Nick spoke. "Do they play the guitar too?" he asked.

Gramps was strumming now.

I thought quickly. "Oh that's just the radio," I stammered. "Mum always listens to it as she cooks."

"Is she burning something?" asked Binni. "I can smell something burning."

There was now a strong burning smell coming from Gramps's garden bonfire. There was a faint whiff of smoke and the sound of wood crackling and flames roaring.

"It's coming from the garden," said Nick.

Then, before I could stop them, they'd pulled back the curtains and what did they see?

Gramps was sitting, strumming his guitar by the light of the bonfire.

His cowboy hat was tipped back. His buckle and spurs gleamed in the firelight. And he was singing.

Yippeeeay ay
Yippee ay ee ee,
Sunny's new friends are here
for tea.
They don't want to meet folk
like me.
So here I am and here I'll stay,
Watching the sun set at the
end of the day.

I looked at my friends.

What were they going to say?

Nick was the first to speak.

"Cool!" he said.

Then Binni. "Mega cool!" she said.

Then Kirsty. "Oh, I see ... the surprise is we're having a campfire tea! With campfire singing! Cool!"

"And a COWBOY!! added Nick. "Extra cool!"

"The cowboy is my grandad," I admitted. "His name is Buffalo Bert."

"Wow! You are so lucky!" said Kirsty.

Soon we all out there eating sausages and beans by the campfire and telling campfire stories and singing campfire songs.

"This is BRILLIANT!" all my friends agreed. "Can we come again?"

That's when Gramps made up a special song for them and they all joined in and then I made up some lines of my own...

I'll sing along and I'll sing out LOUD

'Cos I want to tell my gramps I'm proud.

He's one grandad who really is grand.

He's the best grandad in all the land!

And I love him lots and lots.

About the Author

Michaela Morgan has written over 100 books for children, including the four *Sausage* stories in the Rockets series (A&C Black). She also visits schools for book weeks and speaks at conferences about books and reading.

Michaela lives some of the time in Sussex and some of the time in France. Her hobbies include reading, travelling and daydreaming.

Year 3

Stories with Familiar Settings

Detective Dan • Vivian French

Buffalo Bert • Michaela Morgan

Treasure at the Boot-fair • Chris Powling

Mystery and Adventure Stories

Scratch and Sniff • Margaret Ryan

The Thing in the Basement • Michaela Morgan

On the Ghost Trail • Chris Powling

Myths and Legends

Pandora's Box • Rose Impey

Sephy's Story • Julia Green

Wings of Icarus • Jenny Oldfield